Seeing Eye Willie

by Dale Gottlieb

Alfred A. Knopf
New York

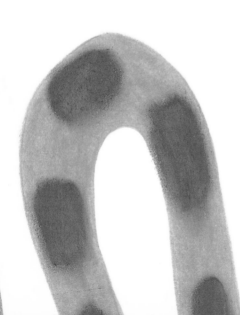

THIS IS A BORZOI BOOK PUBLISHED BY ALFRED A. KNOPF, INC.

Copyright © 1992 by Dale Gottlieb

Library of Congress Cataloging-in-Publication Data
Gottlieb, Dale, 1952–
    Seeing Eye Willie / by Dale Gottlieb.
        p.   cm.
    Summary: A young child gives her own imaginary explanation of how
Willie, a homeless man, came to be the way he is.
    ISBN 0-679-82449-9 (trade) — ISBN 0-679-92449-3 (lib. bdg.)
    [1. Homeless persons—Fiction.]   I. Title.
PZ7.G696Se   1992
[E]—dc20   91-18606

Book design by Edward Miller

Manufactured in the U.S.A.   10 9 8 7 6 5 4 3 2 1

For my parents and brother, Alan, Zelda, and Martin Gottlieb
Thank you, Chris, Blake, and Hill xxxooo
And thanks to my editor, mentor, and friend, Anne Schwartz

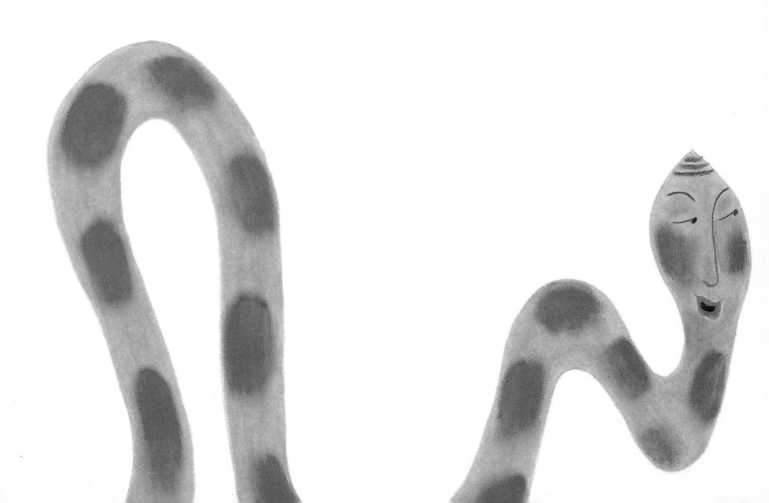

Seeing Eye Willie

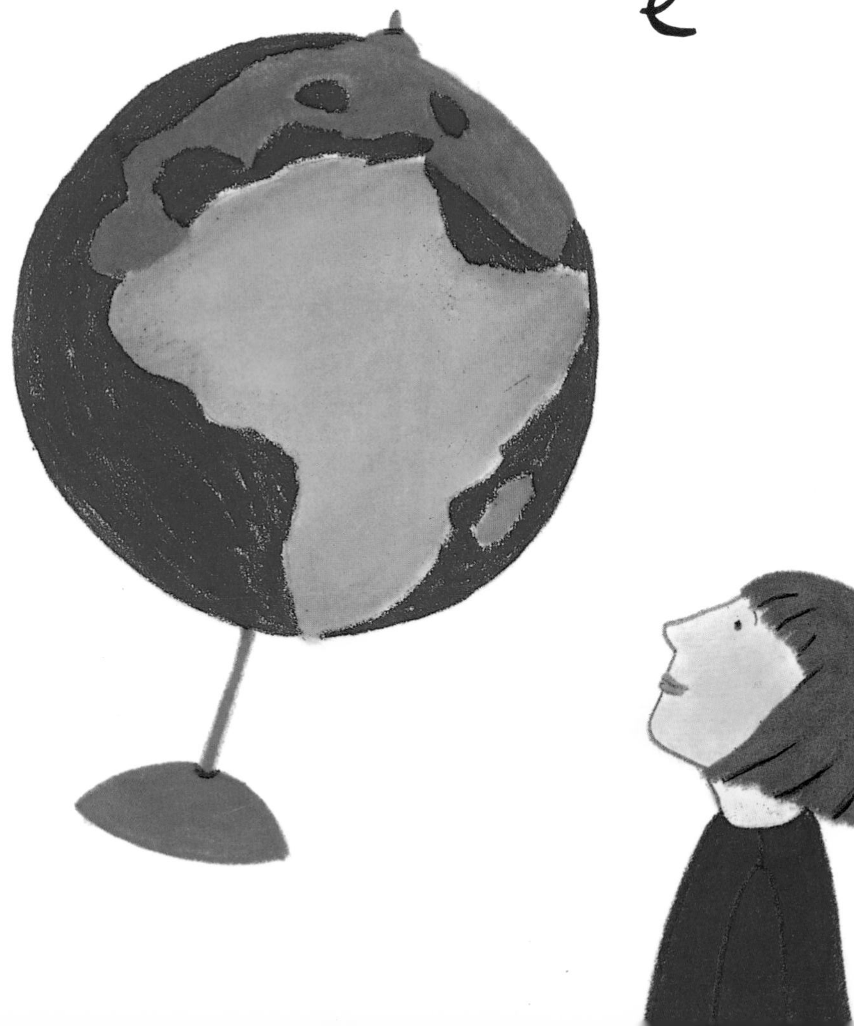

Aunt Augusta, who lives across the street from Spike's Stationery Store, always says, "Willie is like the sun and the moon. He's there when I go to bed at night, and he's there when I wake up in the morning."

She's talking about a skinny old man with a patch over his right eye. His real name is William DuRocher, but most people call him Seeing Eye Willie.

Willie wears embroidered Chinese slippers and an old gray coat, no matter what the weather is. A dried-up snakeskin hangs around his neck, and he's always in front of Spike's, with his flute and his duffel bag by his side.

Stationery
WE HAVE 20 DIFFERENT NEWSPAPERS
IF WE DON'T HAVE IT, YOU DON'T NEED IT
HOT COFFEE
OPEN 24 HOURS

Maybe Seeing Eye Willie doesn't have a home.

Maybe he has no money.

Maybe he doesn't want a home.

Maybe he doesn't want any money.

Maybe he'd like my home.

Maybe he'd like my money.

Maybe the bench in front of Spike's is his home.

Maybe he has **lots** of money.

"Maybe's don't make it so," my mother
says whenever I guess about Willie.

Lots of people think they know what happened
to make William DuRocher the way he is.

Frank, the barber,
says it was the war.

Ethel, from the pharmacy,
says it was a broken heart.

Lou, the butcher, says
it was the Depression.

And Kate, from Toyland, thinks
it was fire that destroyed his
house and took his eye.

But those are all just stories.

I have my own story, and it goes like this:

A long time ago, when Seeing Eye Willie was born, the world was young and small. Willie could crawl around the whole planet in five minutes.

One day when he was in Africa, a lion spotted him. He moved right in front of Baby Willie and roared hello. Baby Willie started to cry.

The lion stretched out his great paws to pick
up the baby. He wanted to hold Willie
and show him there was no reason
to be afraid. But he accidentally
scratched Willie's right eye
and blinded it.

"You think I'm a terrible old hungry thing, don't you? But I'm not!" And he licked Baby Willie's eye till it was healed. Baby Willie stopped crying. His eye didn't hurt anymore and he wasn't afraid.

The lion raised a front paw and reached deep
into his mane. "Here, Willie, this is for you."
And he handed him a wooden flute.
"The music you make will keep you
company." Then the lion
patted Baby Willie and
roared good-bye.

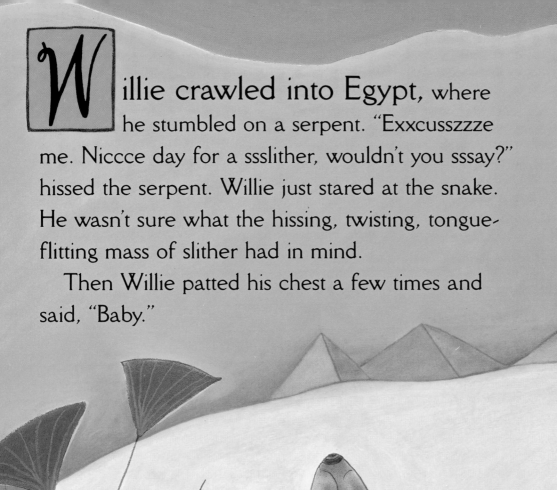

illie crawled into Egypt, where he stumbled on a serpent. "Exxcusszzze me. Niccce day for a ssslither, wouldn't you sssay?" hissed the serpent. Willie just stared at the snake. He wasn't sure what the hissing, twisting, tongue-flitting mass of slither had in mind.

Then Willie patted his chest a few times and said, "Baby."

"Oh," paused the serpent. "Come to think of it, I've never ssseen a baby before. Well, come along. You look ready to go, and ssso am I."

Baby Willie crawled, and the snake seemed to turn inside out with every move. By the time they got to the tip of Mesopotamia, the snake was different.

"Here, Baby, ssshow thisss to your friendsss back home," he said. And he gave Willie the old speckled skin he had shed along the way.

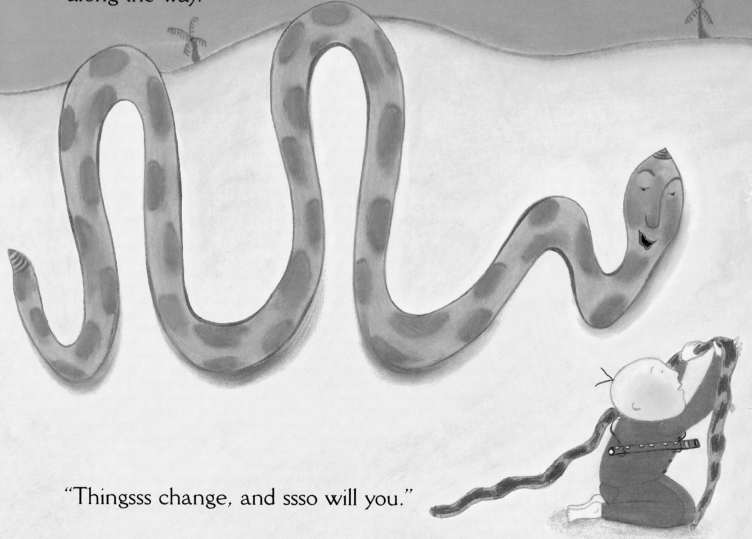

"Thingsss change, and ssso will you."

Baby Willie thanked the snake and waved good-bye as he crawled across the Middle East. People were too busy arguing with each other there to notice him. So he kept going...

...over to India,
where a nice mother
elephant gave him a ride
to the edge of China.

"Good-bye, Baby Willie,"
she trumpeted to him
sweetly. "Remember where
you came from when you use
these." And she gave him a wooden
spoon and a coconut bowl to eat with.

China was big, and Willie crawled and crawled. He heard laughing from behind some trees. When he turned around to listen more closely, a gold-colored monkey carrying a basket sprang right up to his nose. Baby Willie poked his head into the basket. He found food and flowers, and then he found the prize —black silk slippers embroidered with little pictures.

"These
slippers
will grow
with your feet.
They tell the
story of you,"
the monkey said
as he laughed and
jumped around. "Most
creatures' feet tell a story.
Look at mine." And he
rolled himself up like a snail
and showed his wrinkled soles.
Baby Willie looked and looked.
"Funny story," he finally said, which
made the monkey laugh even more. Then
Baby Willie waved good-bye and was gone...

...up to Russia, which seemed to stretch on forever. Willie's teeth chattered and his lips turned blue. A seal spotted him and threw him a coat. "You'll be warm and safe in this," he said.

"Thank you," Baby Willie shivered.

"The pleasure is all mine," answered the seal.

"Home, please," Willie said as he pointed to the east.

"Okay, home. Hop on. I'll swim you to land," said the seal.

When they reached Alaska, they said good-bye.

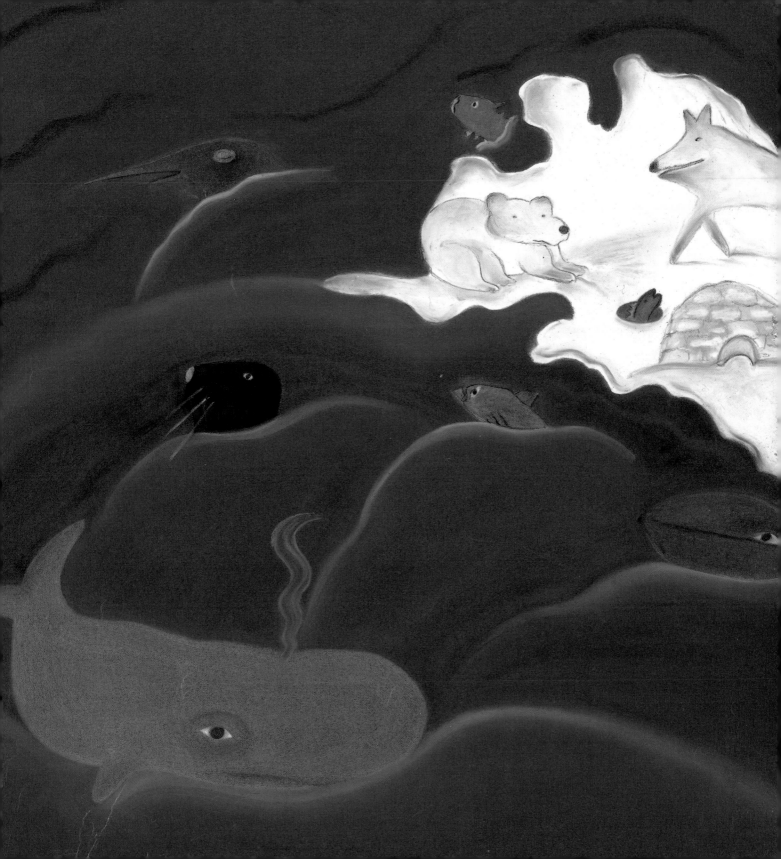

Willie kept on crawling home.

Five minutes later he
was grown up and old.

And that's how **I** see the story of Seeing
Eye Willie. Maybe I'll tell it to him someday.
Or maybe I won't. I don't want to disturb him.

My father says, "I'm sure William DuRocher
has his own story."

Dale Gottlieb

found her inspiration for this book by watching and wondering about homeless people in her neighborhood.

Ms. Gottlieb is the author and illustrator of several books, including *Big Dog* and, most recently, *My Stories by Hildy Calpurnia Rose*. She lives in Bellingham, Washington, with her husband, Chris Hudson, and their two sons, Blake and Hill.

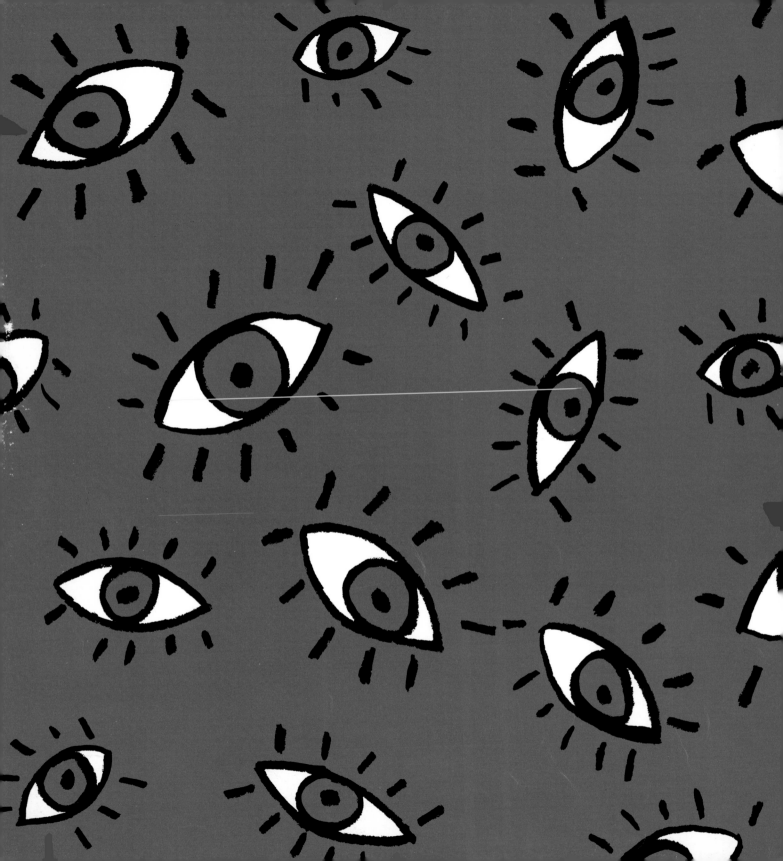